Little Louie
the
Baby Bloomer

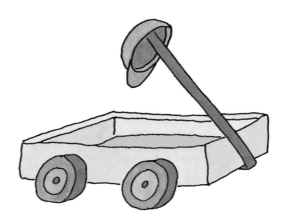

BY ROBERT KRAUS

PICTURES BY JOSE ARUEGO & ARIANE DEWEY

HARPERCOLLINS*PUBLISHERS*

Little Louie the Baby Bloomer
Text copyright © 1998 by Robert Kraus
Illustrations copyright © 1998 by Jose Aruego and Ariane Dewey
Printed in the U.S.A. All rights reserved.
http://www.harperchildrens.com

Library of Congress Cataloging-in-Publication Data
Kraus, Robert, 1925–
    Little Louie the baby bloomer / by Robert Kraus ; pictures by Jose Aruego and Ariane Dewey.
        p.   cm.
    Summary: Leo the tiger worries and wonders why his little brother can't do anything right, but his parents encourage Leo to be patient.
    ISBN 0-06-026293-1. — ISBN 0-06-026294-X (lib. bdg.)
    [1. Tigers—Fiction.   2. Toddlers—Fiction.   3. Brothers—Fiction.]   I. Aruego, Jose, ill.
II. Dewey, Ariane, ill.   III. Title.
PZ7.K868Lit   1998
[E]—DC20
                                                                                96-42434
                                                                                CIP
                                                                                AC

Typography by Al Cetta
1   2   3   4   5   6   7   8   9   10
❖
First Edition

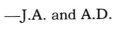

To Alix and Parker

—R.K.

To Juan

—J.A. and A.D.

Leo's little brother, Louie,
couldn't do anything right.

He couldn't throw a ball.

He couldn't pull a wagon.

He couldn't rattle his rattle.

He was a messy eater.

And he never said a word.

Every day Leo played with his friends.

Every day he tried to play with Little Louie, too.

"What's the matter with Little Louie?" asked Plover.

"Why can't he throw a ball?" asked Elephant.

"Why can't he pull a wagon?" asked Crocodile.

"Why can't he rattle his rattle?" asked Snake.

"And he can't talk, either," said Leo.

Leo was worried.

"Why won't Little Louie play with me?"
he asked.

"Little Louie will play with you in his own
good time," said Leo's father.

"And in his own good way," said Leo's mother.

"He's a late bloomer, just like you."

So Leo stopped trying to play with Little Louie
and decided to teach Louie instead.
Every day he showed him how to throw a ball.

Every night he showed him how to pull a wagon.

He showed Louie how to rattle his rattle,

and he tried to teach him how to say his name.

LE+O=LEO
LEE-OOH
LEO   LEOOO

Leo decided not to teach Little Louie how to eat.

"Are you sure Little Louie is a bloomer?"
Leo asked his parents.

"Patience," said his mother.

"A watched bloomer doesn't bloom,"
said his father.

Then one day Leo got it!

Little Louie had bloomed already.

He could throw.

He could pull.

He could rattle.

He could even eat neatly.

He just did it all in his own good way.

The next time Leo's friends came over, Leo said,

"Little Louie made it!"

"Just like you," said Plover.

"A late bloomer," said Crocodile.

"A baby bloomer," Leo said.

"Except he still doesn't talk."

"Leo!" said Little Louie.